Finally, Back To The Ocean

やがて海へ帰る

～ Buddhism For Happiness ～
しあわせになる仏教

本田 つよし

Finally, Back To The Ocean
やがて海へ帰る

~ Buddhism For Happiness ~
しあわせになる仏教

Preface

As mentioned in my first anthology,"Yet The Sky Is Blue", hospitalization and then departure of my father was a trigger for me to become interested in Buddhism. To tell the truth, my mother is a pious follower of Jodo-Shinshu denomination and recites *Shoshinge* at home on the memorial days. In fact there are more than ten belated persons to whom she offers *Shoshinge* or Amida Sutra. So almost once in three days she recites these Shin Buddhism scriptures. However, I have to confess that since hospitalization of my father in 2016, I myself had not been committed to Buddhism. But while learning the Buddhist teachings, I found that it is easier to understand its essence through English rather than through Japanese. As you know, there are lots of technical terms, especially in Chinese character, Kanji, which prevent you from learning. But through English, this problem is solved amazingly with ease in many cases.

Here, I must not forget to mention Kenneth Tanaka Sensei. In fact, the encounter with him was a lucky co-incidence. In 2018, I happened to find his work *"Shinshu Nyūmon"* at BOOK-OFF near my house, and bought it. And I found that this book has an original version in English, "Ocean". Of course, with no hesitation, I purchased "Ocean" at AMAZON. Then again, I happened to know that there was a class "Buddhism through English" at Bukkyo Dendo Kyokai by, surprisingly, Kenneth Sensei himself! Actually, all these things happened almost at the same time. I think Amida guided me to Kenneth Sensei, with the wisdom of hindsight. Anyway, I have been learning the essence of the Buddhist teachings under the guidance of Kenneth Sensei and now I have been able to publish my SECOND anthology in English on Buddhism.

HONDA Tsuyoshi

序文

最初の詩集『それでも空は青い』で触れたように、私が仏教に興味をもったのは、私の父の入院と逝去がきっかけでした。実を言うと、私の母は敬虔な浄土真宗信徒で、命日には家で「正信偈」を唱えています。実際のところ、母が正信偈や阿弥陀経を唱えている故人の数は 10 人以上で、母は三日に一回以上、真宗のお経を唱えていることになるのです。しかしながら、私自身は、2016 年に父が入院するまで仏教に積極的に関わっていなかったことを告白しなければなりません。でも、仏教を勉強するにつれて、日本語より英語で学んだほうが、その本質を理解しやすいということに気がついたのです。ご存じのとおり、仏教にはたくさんの専門用語、とくに漢字の言葉があり、これらが学びを妨げています。ところが、英語を通してなら、多くの場合、この問題は驚くほど簡単に解決してしまいます。

ここで、ケネス田中先生のことに触れないわけにはいきません。実は、先生との出会いは幸運な偶然でした。2018 年、私は自宅近くのブックオフで、先生の書かれた『真宗入門』という本をたまたま見つけて購入しました。そしてこの本には『Ocean』という英語の原書があることを知り、もちろんためらうことな

く、アマゾンで買って取り寄せたのです。そして、またしても偶然に、仏教伝道協会で、「仏教を英語で学ぶ」クラスがあり、それも何とケネス先生が講師であることを知ったのです！　実際、これらのことはすべてほとんど同時に起きました。後から考えてみれば、阿弥陀様のお導きだったのでしょう。ケネス先生のご指導のもと、私は仏教の本質を学び続けており、今、仏教について英語で二冊目の詩集を出版できるまでになったのです。

本田つよし

To My Mother

母へ

Contents

Buddhism For Me

私にとって
仏教はイズムではなく
行動のための指針
議論するためでも
誰かを
裁くためのものでもない

それは幸せのレシピ
ただし
食材を集めて料理するのは
他の誰でもない私
ただ読んだだけでは
幸せという名のご馳走は
運ばれてこないのだ

For me

Buddhism is not an ism.

It is a guidance

For my action,

Neither for argument

Nor for judgement.

It is a recipe for happiness.

However,

It is not someone else

But me who collect ingredients

And cook.

Just reading it will not bring me

A good meal named happiness.

Your Will

あなたの今日の心がけだけが
あなたの明日の幸せを
創りだす
他はない

ブッダが
「清らかな心で話し、
行動すれば
幸せがついてくる」
と言っているように

Just your today's will

Creates

Our tomorrow's happiness,

Nothing else.

As the Buddha says

"If you speak or act

With clear mind,

Happiness follows you." ※

※ "*The Dhammapada*" translated by Valerie J. Roebuck, p.3 Penguin Books

Good Seed

心の中の
善い種に
水やりを続けよう

美しい花が
一日で育ち
咲くことはない

良いことは
時間をかけて起こるが
悪いことが起こるのは
一瞬だ

心の中の
善い種に
水やりを続けよう

Keep watering
The good seed
In your heart.

A beautiful flower
Will not grow and blossom
In a day.

Good things take time
To happen,
While bad things happen
In a moment.

Keep watering
The good seed
In your heart.

The Present Moment

過去と他人を
変えることはできないが
今この瞬間と
自分自身を変えることは
できる

それが
あなたが幸せになる
唯一の方法

You cannot change
The past and others,
But you can change
The present moment
And yourself.

That's the only way
To create happiness
For you.

To Belong Or Not To Belong

何かのグループに
所属している
という感覚は
私の心を安定させるが
同時に私という存在を
か弱いものにする

どのグループにも
所属していない
という感覚は
私の心を自由にするが
同時に私を限りなく
孤独にする

所属するか
所属しないか
人は永遠に
思い悩むのだ

A sense

That I belong to some group

Makes my mind stable,

But at the same time

Makes my presence

Vulnerable.

A sense

That I do not belong to any group

Makes my mind liberated,

But at the same time

Makes myself alone

Boundlessly.

To belong or

Not to belong,

That is the eternal question

For man.

Someone Never Comes

かつて私は
いつか誰かがやって来て
私を幸せにしてくれると
考えていた

でも仏教を学び
実践すればするほど
こういう思いが募っていく

誰かは、来ない
いつかは、来ない

今、私にはわかる
幸せとは
自分の内側からやって来るもの

これ以上望むことがあろうか？

Once I was thinking
Someone would come
To make me happy
Someday.

But the more I have learned
And practiced Buddhism,
The more I am feeling this way.

Someone never comes.
Someday never comes.

Now I know
Happiness comes
From within.

Who could ask for more?

Journey Of Life

人生とは
自分を探し
結局
自分に戻る旅

大きな輪の中で
ぐるりと一回りし
もとにいた場所に帰る

そんな旅なのだ

Life is a journey

To search for yourself

And to get back

To yourself.

You go round

In a big circle

And get back to where you were.

That's the journey of your life.

Well-balanced

純粋すぎることに
注意しよう
危険かもしれないから

良いバランスを心がけ
矛盾するものどうしを
受け入れよう

ときには
二極化しているものを
共存させることも
やってみよう

Beware

Being too purified,

Because it can be dangerous.

Be well-balanced,

And accept things of

Contradiction.

Sometime

Try to make

Two polarized things

Co-exist.

Honesty

最後は
正直が
勝つ

嘘をつくことは
他の誰よりも
自分自身を
滅ぼしてしまうだろう

Honesty is

The best strategy

In the end.

Telling a lie will

Ruin yourself

Rather than

Anyone else.

How To Be Strong

自分の外側にあるもので
強くなろうとしても
きっと
上手く行かないだろう

自分の内側にあるもので
強くなろうとしたとき
とてつもない強さを
ずっと
身につけることが
できるだろう

If you try to be strong

Relying on things

From outside,

You will fail for sure.

If you try to be strong

Relying on things

From inside,

You will get

Tremendous strength

For good.

Weakness

人は
自分自身の
弱さを認めた
その瞬間から
本当に
強くなれる

You can truly

Be strong,

From the moment

You recognize

Your own

Weakness.

Be Satisfied

自分にないものを数えて
悩むのは
止めにしよう

今、自分にあるものを
数えて
満足しよう

Stop counting

What you have not,

And being worried.

Be satisfied

To count.

What you have now.

Those being left behind

先を行く
人たちだけでなく
取り残される
人たちも
気にかけて
いたいと思う

彼らこそ
社会の根幹だ

I would like to

Be concerned

Not only for

Those going ahead

But also for

Those being left behind.

They are

The very basis of society.

People

テクノロジーは
必ずしも
人を幸せにしない

便利さは
必ずしも
人を幸せにしない

宗教は
必ずしも
人を幸せにしない

人を
幸せにするのは
その人自身だ

Technology
Does not necessarily
Make people happy.

Convenience
Does not necessarily
Make people happy.

Religion
Does not necessarily
Make people happy.

It's people
Who make themselves
Happy.

For Others

あなた自身のために
生きるとき
人生は幸せなものとなる

そして
誰かのために
生きるとき
あなたの人生は
最も幸せになる

Life can be happy

When it is lived

For yourself.

And

It can be

Most happy

When it is lived

For others.

Action With Love

かつて私は
愛とは何かを知りたかった

でも今では
愛とは何か気にならない

私は愛で何ができるかを
気にしたいのだ

「愛」という言葉が
私を迷わせるのなら
あえてこの言葉から
距離を置こう
そのかわりに
言葉でなく行動によって
生きていくのだ

Once I was wondering
What love is.

But now I don't care for
What love is.

I'd like to care for
What I can do with love.

When the word "love"
Makes me confused,
I dare to stay away
From this word.
Instead
I live with action
Rather than with words.

Everything In Your Heart

人は
すべてを心に抱いて
生まれる

すべての知識
すべての理解
そしてすべての智慧

教育とは
これらを
再確認することなのだ

You are born
With everything
In your heart.

Every knowledge,
Every understanding,
And every wisdom.

To educate yourself is
To re-confirm
These things.

Truth

生まれる前から
そのことは
わかっていた

I knew it

Before

I was born.

Truth Of Life

世界中の
あらゆる参考書や
辞書を調べても
インターネットで
何時間検索しても
人生の真実には
たどりつけないかも
しれない

だけど
毎日を暮らす
あなた自身の中から
人生の真実は
ひょっこりと
見つかることが
あるのだ

ノーベル賞受賞者よりも
隣のラーメン屋の
主人のほうが

You might not reach

To the truth of life

Even looking up in

Every reference book

And every dictionary

Around the world,

Or by hours of searching

In the Internet.

However,

The truth of life

Could pop out

From yourself

And be found

While you live

A daily life.

A master of

The next door Ramen shop

ずっとわかっていたりする

それが
人生の真実というものだ

Understands it far more than
A Nobel laureate.

That's what
The truth of life is.

The Present Moment

過去の
すべての出来事は
今この瞬間に

今この瞬間は
未来の
あらゆる可能性に向かって
開かれている

今あなたに
起きていることはすべて
宇宙の始まり以来
何十億年の出来事の
結果であり
今あなたが行うことが
これからの宇宙を
創ってゆく

すべては
今この瞬間

All what happened

In the past

Have been connected to

The present moment

Which is

Open to

Every possibility

In the future.

All what happen to you now

Are the outcome of

What happened

In the billions of years

Since the beginning of the universe,

And what you do now

Will create

The tomorrow universe.

All that matters is

The present moment.

今、行動を

Do it now.

Simple Buddhist Practice

良く聞く

今やる

思いやる

Listen well.

Do it now.

Care for others.

Horizontal and Vertical

人生に横の軸しか
持たない人は
いつまでも
果てしない荒野を
彷徨うが
_{さまよ}

心に縦の軸を
持つ人は
いつでも
大いなる存在へ
宇宙へ
つながることができる

Those who only have

Horizontal axis in their lives,

Would be wandering

Around the boundless wild

Forever.

Yet those who have

Vertical axis in their hearts,

Could be connected

To the Great Being

To the universe

Anytime.

One Great Circle

アミダがあなたを抱くとき
あなたもアミダを抱きしめる

アミダはあなたを包み込む
やさしく大きな両腕で

あなたの力は抜けてゆく
その身をアミダに任せてる

ひとつの大きな輪の中で

When Amida holds you,
You too hold Amida tight.

Amida wraps up you
With his great gentle arms.

You let yourself go
And leave your whole being to Amida,

In One Great Circle.

Shinran

もうひとりのイエスに
なることはできない

もうひとりの釈尊に
なることもできない

でも
もしかしたら
もうひとりの親鸞には
なれるかもしれない

例えば「私は念仏を称えましても
天に踊り地に踊る歓喜の心が
ありません。また、浄土に
早く往きたい心も起きません。
これは、どういうわけで
ありましょう」と尋ねられて
親鸞は「親鸞も同じ不審を
懐いていた」
と答えている※

You cannot be
A Jesus Christ.

You cannot be
A Shakyamuni Buddha, either.

However,
You could be
A Shinran
By some chance.

For example,
Asked "Although I say the nembutsu,
I feel no leaping, dancing joy.
Also, I have no wish to hurry
To the Pure Land.
Why is this?"
Shinran replied,
 "The very same thought
Has struck me." ※

何という答！

これが
誰にでもわかる
親鸞の凄さだ

※『歎異抄をひらく』高森顕徹　p.86（１万年堂出版）
"Unlocking Tannisho" Kentetsu Takamori, p.8 Ichimannendo Publishing

What an extraordinary answer this is!

This is what makes

Everyone see

How amazing Shinran is.

Faith

だから、信じる
だけど、信じる

<ruby>一<rt>いち</rt>途<rt>ず</rt></ruby>に信じることは
素晴らしい
でも、疑うことは
自然

だから、信じる
だけど、信じる

どちらがスピリチュアルか
どちらが人間的か
簡単に答えは出ない

だから、信じる
だけど、信じる

私の思いは
揺れている

So, I have faith.
Yet, I have faith.

Having faith single-mindedly
Is wonderful.
Yet, having doubt
Is natural.

So, I have faith.
Yet, I have faith.

Which is spiritual?
Which is human-like?
No easy answer.

So, I have faith.
Yet, I have faith.

My mind is swinging
Between them.

Caring For My Mother

母が倒れた
躊躇する間もなく
私は
母を介護する立場になった

母はずっと
誰かを世話してきた人だ
母が世話した人は
みんな
長生きしている

功徳を積んだ
母は
きっとお浄土へ
往生するだろう

では
母を世話している私は
往生できるだろうか？

My mother collapsed.
Without a time of hesitation
I have become
The one who cares for her.

My mother has been
The one who cares for someone.
All those who were cared for
By my mother
Lived long.

Having accumulated virtues,
My mother definitely
Will be reborn
In the Pure Land.

Then,
Could I who am caring for her
Be reborn in the Pure Land?

もしかしたら
母が倒れたのは
私に功徳を積ませ
往生させるためかもしれない

ありがたや　ありがたや

Maybe

My mother collapsed

To let me accumulate virtues

And be reborn in the Pure Land.

How grateful I feel!

Cycle Of Dependence

赤ちゃんの時
私の命はすべて
母親にかかっていた

今、私に介護されて
母親の命は
私の手にかかっている

誰かに頼り
そしていずれ誰かに
頼られる人になる

生きるとは
頼り頼られるの繰り返しなのだ

When I was a baby,
My life was totally
Dependent on my mother.

Now being cared for by me,
My mother's life is
Dependent on me.

Dependent on someone
And then being one
Who someone is dependent on.

To live is
The cycle of dependence.

Presence

あなたが存在することが
私が存在することに
必要不可欠

私が存在することが
あなたが存在することに
必要不可欠

そうやって私たちは
この奇跡的な世界に
生きている

Your presence is
Indispensable
To my presence.

My presence is
Indispensable
To your presence.

That's the way
We are alive
In this miraculous world.

Family

人として生まれ
父親から
智慧を学び
母親から
思いやりを学ぶ

気づいていても
いなくても
家族とはそういうものだ

Being born as a human,

You will have learned

Wisdom from your father,

And compassion

From your mother.

Whether you have noticed it or not,

That's the way

A family is.

Diligence

私が両親に
最も感謝しているのは
二人とも
勤勉な人であったことだ

困難に出会った時
私がへこたれず
すべてをやり直して
立ち直れたのは

両親から学んだ
勤勉さのおかげなのだ

日本人の多くが
私の言っていることに
共感してくれると
思う

What I thank my parents
Most for is
That they were both
Diligent people.

Whenever I have faced with difficulties,
I never gave in and
Could do it all again
And rise.

That's thanks to the diligence
Learned from my parents.

I think
Many Japanese will have
Sympathy
With what I'm saying.

Aging

年齢<ruby>をとるとは

赤ちゃんになるようなこと

もともと出て来たところへ

帰ってゆくこと

Aging is like

Becoming a baby,

And getting back to

Where we came from.

Finally, Back To The Ocean

時間という
川の流れに乗って
やがて私は
海へ帰る

そこで私は命の源（みなもと）へ
溶け込んでゆく

私が海になり
海が私になる

私の意志は海の意志

それは
すべてが私の思い通りになる
という意味ではなく
「思い通り」と思う私が溶けて
海とひとつになるのだ

Riding on the flow of river
Which is time,
I will get back to the ocean
In the end.

There the origin of my life
Into which I will be dissolved.

I become the ocean
And the ocean becomes me.

My will is the will of the ocean.

It means
Not that everything will go as I wish
But that I who wish "as I wish"
Will be dissolved
And become One with the ocean.

HONDA Tsuyoshi
本田 つよし

Profile
プロフィール

Born in Kumamoto Prefecture. Graduated from Waseda University.
熊本県生まれ。早稲田大学第一文学部英文学科卒業。

Weblog "English for Happiness"
ブログ「しあわせになる英語」
https://www.englishforhappiness.com/

Twitter
ツイッター
https://twitter.com/englishforhapp

A member of the Steering Committee of "Sangha for Studying and Practicing Buddhism Through Basic English"
「仏教を初歩英語で学び実践するサンガの会」運営委員

Finally, Back To The Ocean
やがて海へ帰る
〜 Buddhism For Happiness 〜
しあわせになる仏教

発行日　　2021 年 11 月 1 日　第 1 刷発行

著者　　　本田 つよし（ほんだ・つよし）

発行者　　田辺修三
発行所　　東洋出版株式会社
　　　　　〒 112-0014　東京都文京区関口 1-23-6
　　　　　電話　03-5261-1004（代）　振替　00110-2-175030
　　　　　http://www.toyo-shuppan.com/

印刷・製本　　日本ハイコム株式会社